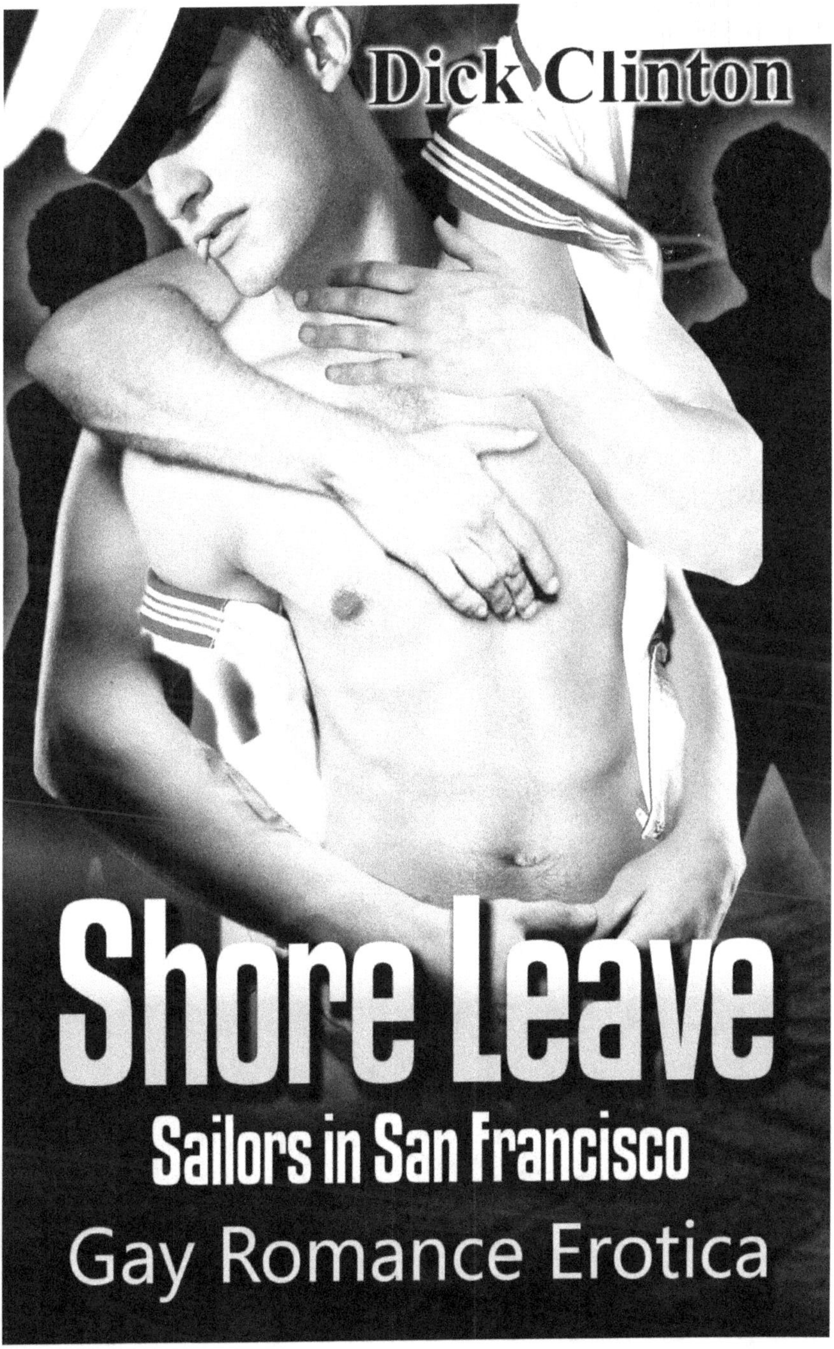

Dick Clinton

Shore Leave

Sailors in San Francisco

Gay Romance Erotica

WARNING

This book contains sexually explicit scenes and adult language. It may be considered offensive to some readers. This book is for sale to adults ONLY.

* * * * * * * * * * * * * * * * * * *

Please store your files wisely where they cannot be accessed by underage readers.

Please feel free to send me an email. Just know that these emails are filtered by my publisher. Good news is always welcome.

Dick Clinton - **dick_clinton@awesomeauthors.org**

About the Publisher

4Fun Publishing, a member of **BLVNP Incorporated**, 340 S. Lemon #6200, Walnut CA 91789, info@blvnp.com / legal@blvnp.com

NOTE: Due to the highly emotional reaction of some people to works of erotic fiction, any email sent to the above address that contains foul language or religious references is automatically deleted by our anti-spam software and will not be seen. All other communications are welcome.

DISCLAIMER

Please don't be stupid and kill yourself. This book is a work of FICTION. Do not try any new sexual practice that you find in this book. It is fiction and not to be confused with reality. Neither the author nor the publisher or its associates assume any responsibility for any loss, injury, death or legal consequences resulting from acting on the contents in this book. Every character in this book is over 18 years of age. The author's opinions are not to be construed as the opinions of the publisher. The material in this book is for entertainment purposes ONLY. Enjoy.

Shore Leave

Sailors in San Francisco
Gay Romance Erotica

By: Dick Clinton

ISBN: 978-1-62761-774-1

Part 1
Let's Go Hustle Some Queers

Our ship had recently docked at Alameda Naval Base in California after being on maneuvers in the Pacific for several weeks. The crew was in high spirits because the captain had given us a 3-day shore leave pass. San Francisco Bay was an excellent liberty port. It had many things to see and do and the girls were more than happy to show a lonely service man a good time. It was my first time going ashore on the West Coast and I was excited about my leave.

A man can get particularly horny being away from sexual partners for this length of time. I had turned 19 this past month and still at that age where I was horny most of the time. Half of the young crew walked around with a boner. At 6 feet tall, I was more than physically fit with an excellent body, thick blond hair and deep blue eyes. I was also hung like a stud horse. I had an unusually large, thick, eleven-inch cock, big and low hanging balls, and a nice firm butt. I liked sex.

I would masturbate as many as four or five times a day and night if I could find some private place to jack off. Sex, for me, released stress and tension. Besides, it just felt so damn good. It was difficult to find a private place aboard the ship, where a guy could drop a load. I noticed other men didn't seem to care if others knew they were whacking their 'pud,' but I guess I was a private person. I'd come upon mates masturbating together in the showers, and the head, and heard rumours of 'circle jerks' taking place in various areas of the ship. I had no objection to their activities, because I knew it was just a natural sexual thing to do.

I have several good buddies aboard the ship so when we had 'leave' we would go ashore together as a group to find some pussy. This time they said they were going to 'hustle some queers' to get some extra spending money. They would hustle their bodies to get a queer to blow them, get their rocks off, and get paid for it. I was still naive about such matters, but that sounded reasonable to me. I'd never had a queer blow me, but getting my rocks off and getting paid for it, sounded like a good deal to me. I didn't know how to manage this, but I thought I'd observe my more experienced buddies to learn how this was done.

"Mike, are you ready to get laid?" one of my buddies yelled at me as we headed down the gangplank to the dock.

"Let's go find some queers first. Frisco is full of hungry fags just waiting to service a hot sailor," another of my buddies said.

There were usually four of us in our little "gang" that had become friends. We headed for the nearest bus stop to catch a ride to the San Francisco bus terminal then board a local bus to Market Street where most of the fags hung out to pick up sailors.

"Come on, Mike," Jack said as he motioned for me to follow him. "We'll show you how to make some money with that big cock of yours."

I knew my dick was quite a bit larger than those of most of the men on the ship, because when we were taking our showers together they would tease me. They would say they dared not drop the soap around me. They didn't want that monster up their ass. I'd just smiled with pride and shook it at them in jest. Some of the men would stare at my cock admiringly. I would often turn away because I found myself getting aroused from the men watching me. I had to admit I had an unusually big cock and a nice set of balls and tonight on my shore leave I was going to try to flaunt it to make money.

"Just sit here at the bus stop and a fag will come by and ask if you want to take a ride," Jack told me. "Then you hop in the car. The fag will want to 'feel you up', and you'll say, 'If you want my cock, you'll have to pay for it.' He'll drive you to a secluded spot and blow you. The usual price is about $20.00 or so. He'll drop you off back here and then you can go have a good time."

It sounded kind of peculiar to me but I would give it a try. The other men spread out in different sections of the area to get picked up. We were to gather back here in about an hour. I felt a little self-conscious sitting there like a piece of meat. Well I guess that's what I was exposing, my 'piece of meat.' I wasn't sure if I could do this. Just the thought of another man touching my cock was weird to me. I didn't want the other 'swabbies' to think I was chicken, so I reluctantly spread my legs to give the fags a better look at my crotch and rubbed it a few times to get it semi-hard for exhibit.

I notice the same car pass me two times in the last few minutes. I looked at the driver and thought he was checking me out. What could I do to let him know I was ready for some action? I leaned back on the bench and spread my legs to show off my cock in my tailored whites. I guess it worked because on the third time around the block he pulled into the curb and stopped the car, rolled down the window, and spoke to me.

"Hello. Would you like to go for a ride?" he asked.

"Sure." I said as I opened the car door and hopped in the front seat next to him.

I looked back to see if my buddies saw me making contact but Tex was talking with some female on the sidewalk. He didn't see me get in the car. Perhaps this was a mistake. What am I, a male whore? Trying to sell my body just like that female whore? I couldn't back out now because we were pulling away from the curb.

"They call me 'Butch'. What is your name?" he said.

I had to smile at the name. ' Butch.' Although he did look rather straight.

"I'm Mike and I'm looking for a good time," I said rather nervously. Might as well get this action going, I thought to myself.

Butch looked at me with a rather surprised look and said, "Okay. That sounds cool. I have a place nearby we can use. It's in an old deserted warehouse. It's a good place for some action. That okay with you?" he asked.

I nodded agreeably as he drove down the street. We went into an older section of the city by the waterfront, driving past several deserted buildings and warehouses until we pulled up at a large dark building. Stopping in front of some large warehouse doors, Butch got out, opened the doors and we drove in. It was quiet and dark except for the car lights. He stopped the car and turned off the motor.

I was getting nervous about this. What if this guy was a 'psycho' of some sort and wanted to cut me up? Oh boy! How do I get out of this one?

He opened his door and told me to stand by the car. He walked up to me slowly and placed his hand on my crotch. I was too nervous to get hard but as he rubbed my crotch area my cock started to firm up. Maybe this dude wasn't so bad after all. He slowly began to unbutton my uniform and reach inside my pants to find my hardening cock. I was beginning to relax now.

I'd never had a man touch my cock before. He gently caressed my cock as I began to stiffen. He dropped to his knees and started feeling and examining my privates. He placed his mouth to the head of my uncircumcised cock head and eased his tongue under my sensitive foreskin. It was an amazing, sensuous feeling. He licked the pre-cum slowly oozing from my cock. He explored my balls and nuzzled them in his mouth. He was excellent. I was beginning to think I might enjoy this after all, even if it was a man sucking on me. I closed my eyes to fantasize that it was some girl sucking my cock instead.

I was not aware of anything around me until suddenly someone rushed from the other side of the car and grabbed me.

"What the fuck?" I yelled out. Butch yanked my pants down my legs, causing me to lose my balance. A third man grabbed my other arm as I struggled to hit them and get away.

"Let me go, you fagots! I'll beat the crap out of you. Let me go!" I shouted but by then, they had me secure. They pulled my hands behind my back, placed handcuffs on me, and shoved me against the car. Another man placed some tape across my mouth so I couldn't yell. I was angry and petrified at the same time. What the hell was going on?

"Calm down, Mike. We're not going to harm you," Butch assured me. "In fact we're planning to give you plenty of enjoyment, but you must co-operate. Calm down, calm down.

"Now let's just go to our little game room, our game room of pleasure."

I was still struggling as I was forced to walk to the end of the warehouse where I was led up a small flight of stairs onto a small platform or loading dock. They forced me to face the wall and tied my legs with leather straps. They took the handcuffs off and put my arms in leather slings and secured my wrists.

I couldn't get loose no matter how hard I tried. I was under their control and was spread eagle and strapped to a cross. My shirt top and pants remained but my pants had fallen below my knees. My skivvies and T-shirt still remained and needless to say, my cock was not hard anymore. I was terrified. What kind of sick game were they playing with me? I tried to yell and curse back at my captors, but to no avail. I felt someone approach, and then Butch spoke to me in a quiet gentle voice.

"Mike. Relax! We're not going to hurt you, believe me," Butch said as he walked behind me.

He began touching my body. He pulled down my skivvies, and started rubbing my exposed buttocks. I was not enjoying this at all. I froze when Butch took a knife and slowly cut my skivvies from my body. The sound of the knife slicing through the material of my skivvies sent waves of dread through me. What if they started to slice me?

"If you don't want us to mess up your whites you must relax while we take off your pants and top. Do you agree?"

I nodded yes. Butch motioned for his two escorts to remove my leg straps and remove my shoes and whites. My shorts had been cut in half and lay at my feet. They turned me around after releasing my wrist from the straps and pulled my jumper over my head. They tied me up again only face out. I was now completely naked.

"What a nice specimen we have secured here?" Butch said as he looked me up and down. "You are a handsome young sailor chap with a perfect body, fine firm ass, and a magnificent large cock. We are well pleased."

I looked at him more closely for the first time. He was a strikingly handsome man about 35 years old with a dark trim beard and penetrating eyes. He was dressed in full leather chaps, with no front or back and black boots. His large wielding dick hung freely from the opening of his chaps. He wore an open leather vest that left his well-developed chest and torso bare

A spotlight glared in my eyes, making it difficult to see anything other than what was directly in front of me, but I sensed the presence of other people. Butch began massaging some body oil on my shoulders, arms, down my chest and torso until he completely covered my whole body including my cock and my balls.

It was very sensual and I started to get aroused again. He took the tape off my mouth and said if I did not yell he would leave it off. I nodded yes. Here I was, naked, strapped to a cross while a strange man was rubbing oil over every inch of my body. I was wondering what he had in store for me, now that I was completely at his mercy. I began to relax, thinking I might enjoy this after all.

Butch stood in front of me admiring my handsome, masculine body and big, uncut cock. The oil treatment caused my body to glisten and emphasize my rippling stomach muscle. He seemed pleased with his new captive. The cock hanging from his open chaps was becoming aroused. His member was as big as, or possibly even bigger than mine. Butch's escorts moved into the shadows of the darkened room.

"I am going to stimulate your inner desire to be punished by whipping you." He quickly snapped a large leather strap across my body.

It was so unexpected and surprising I took a deep breath, but did not cry out. He struck me again. This time the strap wrapped around my body and stung my bare ass. Then again and again, each time a might bit harder. He was very careful not to hit my privates or leave any marks on my body. I gnawed on my lip as he whipped me and became aware that the sensation was beginning to arouse me. My cock was hardening and extending to its full length. Then he stopped striking me. I took a deep breath and felt my body burning with heated stimulation.

Butch secured my hard throbbing cock in his leather-gloved hands. He placed his mouth over my cock and started engulfing it with extensive, full deep throat action. I'd never felt such a sensation. I desperately wanted him to take me all the way and make me cum. My balls were stirring and ready to release a much needed orgasm. I was reaching the ultimate peak as my cock throbbed with pleasure. I was begging and ready to shoot my load when he suddenly stopped. I leaned forward trying to get him to suck me more. My hard cock was throbbing in mid-air. I pleaded.

"Make me cum. Please. I need release. Please finish me off." Butch got back in a standing position and looked into my eyes.

"Repeat after me. Please make me cum SIR."

I responded quickly. "Please make me cum, SIR. Please, SIR!"

He stood calmly with a smirk on his face. I was out of control. I was going to cum with or without him touching me. My body trembled as my cock jumped and throbbed. I couldn't stop it. I desperately wanted to grab my dick and jack off, or better still have his warm mouth on me once again. I started to cum anyway. My balls ached from my confined sperm. My cock released an uncontrollable spout of cum into the air.

"I'm cumming! I'm cumming! Oh my god, I'm cumming!" I yelled as I strive for sexual release.

My body trembled and spasms of contentment were released from me. Butch was in the line of fire as my cum came gushing from my cock. It shot through the air and saturated his face and chest. I must have shot off about 8 or 10 streams of cum. The last of the oozing cum dripped from the head of my cock, down my shaft, over my balls and to my feet. I lowered my head and took another deep sigh of relief. I had emptied my balls. I felt so relieved. That was hell. I think Butch had enjoyed my torment.

Most of my cum had drenched his body. He rubbed some cum from his sweaty body and placed it to my lips. I tried to resist, but he forced me to taste my own cum and his body sweat. It wasn't as gross as I thought and I soon found myself licking and searching his hands for more cum. Then the remainder of the cum he rubbed on my chest and stomach. I still remained tied to the cross, helpless but relaxed. I assumed he would release me now and let me go.

Butch untied my wrist and legs and told me to sit on a wooden stool that was placed in front of me. I was pleased to get those straps off and to sit. One of his assistants brought out two leather straps with leather fasteners and placed them around both ankles then locked them. I could only move a few feet away from the wall. I was tied up like a wild animal. I was given a bottle of water and left to rest. Butch placed a leather mask over my eyes. I tried to pull it off but was warned that my hands would be tied up again if I resisted. I was to stand while the stool was being removed.

"I've told you Mike, we will not harm you, only give you pleasure. Now relax."

He rubbed his hands over my red, sensitive ass. I tightened my butt cheeks but he slapped my butt and told me to relax. He dropped to his knees and began kissing my ass. He ran his tongue up and down my ass crack and then I felt his warm tongue penetrating me. It was a new feeling to be tongue fucked. My cock started to get hard again. I started stroking my cock while anticipating whatever sex game I was about to experience next.

I continued jacking on my cock while Butch continued tongue fucking my virgin ass. It was relaxing and sensual. I liked it. He leaned me forward. I bend over to give him better access to my anus. He withdrew his tongue and inserted a harder object into my hole. It was not his finger but something much larger. He pulled it out and put it back in again but this time it went much deeper into my ass hole. It touched something inside me and caused my cock rise to the new awareness.

"What the hell is that?" I asked.

"I just placed a large butt plug in your ass. It's there for good reasons so relax and enjoys the feeling." It did feel different but now I was growing accustomed to it.

I became aware of more people gathering around me. They began rubbing my chest and massaging me. Some were now licking my chest and tonguing my hard nipples. Someone was licking under my armpits and licking away my body sweat. My feet, ankles, and toes were being kissed and licked. Hands caressed my buttocks while others sucked, nibbled, and chewed on my nipples.

My whole body was being worshiped and I loved it. I kept jacking on my cock until someone started caressing and kissing it with their hands and mouth while licking and sucking the remains of my cum from my last orgasm from it. He rotated his tongue under my foreskin, cleaning my cock head. I just placed my hands on my hips and let them devour me. I was in complete ecstasy.

While my body went into complete submission to my body worshipers, I felt another warm body pushing against my cock. Some of my body worshipers moved away but someone was guiding my hard cock to a new awareness. I reached forward to discover a set of firm buttocks pressing against my cock.

I held on to his buttocks while my cock worshiper guided my cock into his warm asshole. It was difficult to insert my 11-inch cock into the warm aperture. I knew it was hurting him but I was so horned up I could not care less. I wanted to plant my hard dick into his warm love canal. He cried out in pain as the head of my cock started to enter. Then I plunged all the way in. The person tried to pull away from my penetrating hard cock, but I seized their hips until they relaxed and let out a low whimper of satisfaction.

His ass had received my full shaft. I'd never fucked an ass before. This felt better than any pussy I'd ever entered. It was warm and tight. The sensation was fantastic. My body trembled for a moment as I enjoyed this new and wonderful experience of pleasure. I paused to let my penetrating cock get used to its new surroundings. I did not want to cum too quickly and I wanted to let my receiver get used to my love shaft. I let his ass hole relax then I started to move in and out of this warm ass. It was tight and the grip was so pleasing to my cock.

I began to fuck his ass while my nipples were being tweaked upon. The sweat from my hairy armpits was being savored by a body worshiper's tongue while another was now licking away at my balls. The butt plug in my ass was rubbing against my prostate and I knew my balls were about to release its spunk into his tight warm ass. I wanted to delay my orgasm and continue to enjoy this new experience. I held on to his hips while my 11 inches of manhood filled every crevice of his fuck canal.

I fucked him as long as I could without cumming. He was going into spasms of enjoyment as I massaged his prostate with my dick. He deserved a good fuck from me. I pulled my cock almost all the way out and then shoved it all the way in. I was beginning to enjoy it. We worked together into the final round of an animalistic orgasmic crescendo. I could no longer control my orgasm and began to empty my load deep into my partner's body.

I yanked roughly on his hips and shoved in deep and hard. The sound of my balls were slapping hard against his butt cheeks. My ball licker was going feral as the love juices were oozing from his ass and dripping from my cock and into his mouth. My armpits were dripping with sweat and my nipples were still being sucked on. I could only think of shooting my load into this tight warm pussy ass. I wanted to be completely satisfied and enjoy this fuck. My ass muscles tightened around the butt plug massaging my prostate. That did it. My cock started to shoot load after load, gush after gush of cum into his asshole.

"Ah fuck, I'm cumming. Damn. I'm cumming. Aw shit. I'm cumming." I shouted. The muscles of his ass tighten around my cock, demanding to draw every drop of my love juices deep into the warmth of his receptive body.

This set off a round of sexual frenzy and triggered the others around me. The two men on each side of me were jacking off and streams of cum were shooting from them and onto my body. The ball licker continued his uncontrollable licking and sucking on my nuts while sucking in the ass juices being expelled from my fuck partner.

Someone was licking near my cock shaft as the cum oozed out of his asshole and down into his mouth. The final crescendo of my orgasm was another ball draining load, and to top things off, as I was cumming someone pulled the butt plug out of my ass causing me to yell again with delight. I thought I would pass out with the unbelievable force of my orgasm.

Sweat was running down my face from under the mask. Several of the body worshipers were continuing to lick the sweat and cum from my body. I just relaxed and let them clean me with their tongues. Reluctantly I felt my fuck partner withdrawing and my cock made a slurping sound as it left his anus. My cock was dripping with cum but someone quickly started licking all the cum and ass juices from my cock and balls cleaning inside of my foreskin.

Then when everyone seemed satisfied and had withdrawn, fresh warm, moist towels were being rubbed all over my body. Butch unsnapped my leather mask and pulled it off my head. I could feel the cool rush of air hit my face as Butch wiped my face and forehead and dried my hair with the towel. He looked at me with a grin on his face and commented.

"See, now? That didn't hurt too much, did it?"

Part 2
Thank You Sir!

I looked around to discover that Butch was the only one in sight. All of my body worshipers, and the pussy ass, were gone. As I began to focus my eyes, I noticed a large leather barrel had been rolled onto the platform by two helpers. I leaned on it, catching my breath and relaxed. I was handed another bottle of water and a toke on the joint he was smoking. I took a deep toke and looked at Butch.

"Thank you, SIR!" I said as he tilted his head, looking at my semi-hard cock. "Now can I go?" I asked.

Butch snarled at me and said, "May I go now, SIR."

"O.K.," I snarled back. "May I go now, SIR?"

"NO!" he said and walked away from me.

Two of the helpers unlatched my wall straps and crossed them over me to the opposite side. This forced me to turn around facing the leather covered barrel. The straps were tightened thus pulling my legs further apart. I lost my balance and fell face down lengthwise over the barrel with my ass facing the opposite direction. The helpers secured my wrist straps again and roughly pulled them to the attachments on the wall. I fell over the barrel with my ass in the air.

"Oh no! I'm not going to be fucked. I'm nobody's punk boy," I said out loud. "Let me loose, you cock suckers, let me loose. The butt plug was all right after I got used to it, but no fucking way is a cock going into my virgin ass. No way!"

I struggled, once again trying to release myself from my bondage. Butch came up behind me and slapped my butt hard with his hand. He took the strap he had used earlier and smacked me across my bare butt. I yelled in pain.

"You son of a bitch. That hurt like hell! Fuck you!" I shouted at him.

Without saying a word, he approached me once again. I tensed, expecting another belt strapping, but instead I felt a hot moist breath over my tingling butt cheeks and then Butch's stanched tingling as he kissed each cheek of my ass. He dropped to his knees and placed his tongue into my asshole. I relaxed as I figured that I had no choice but to let him have access to my ass. His tongue fucked me for a few moments then he withdrew his warm wet tongue and I felt another foreign object touching my asshole. It was another butt plug, only this one felt much bigger than the first one he had removed from me earlier. He lubricated it then began to place it into my hole. It hurt at first as it stretched my asshole, yet the slight pain turned quickly to pleasure. It felt damn good.

He slowly moved it in and twisted it around and around, opening and relaxing the inside layer of my ass. I tried to relax and loosen up and enjoy the sensation, but when it was all the way in, I thought that once again I might cum from the amazing sensations it was creating inside of me.

Part of the barrel opened and a large hole opened beneath my cock. Someone inside the barrel gently pulled my cock and balls into the open space. They fondled, kissed, licked and lovingly sucked and worshiped my cock. Suddenly, there were helpers everywhere, my feet were being braced on a leaning platform while at the same time soft, foam-padded leather pillows were being placed under my chest and body. I was being made comfortable but for what reason?

While I was enjoying my cock being sucked through the hole and I was enjoying the feeling of the plug in my stretching asshole, a small part of me was still nervous about what was going on but that was getting less important by the moment I was becoming excited again. Butch gave me another puff on his joint. I could not help but notice his magnificent cock as it hung only a few inches from my face. It was so perfect looking. It had a large tulip shaped head hidden under his lacy foreskin. It hung down a good 7 or 8 inches semi-hard. His balls were covered with a soft fuzz of dark hair. He wore a large silver cock ring around his balls at the base of his cock. I inhaled the pheromones of his manly musk, sweat, and leather. The head of his piss slit had produced a clear pearl of pre-cum. I took another deep whiff of him and realized that I had an uncontrollable desire to touch him, but I was still tightly secured. I stretched my neck toward his cock as he slowly moved toward my mouth.

He placed the head of his cock on my lips. I stuck out my tongue to taste the pre-cum slowly oozing from his piss slot. It was my first taste of man juices, except for my own. It had a pleasant sweet taste with just a slight hint of his body sweat. He smelled of leather and of man. I leaned my head towards him and licked his sweet pre-cum covered cock. I opened wider, eager to suck his cock into my mouth. I tongued under his foreskin to taste even more delightful smegma. He progressively got hard. I was impressed and amazed at the size of his splendid cock. Meanwhile my cock was still being sucked on, in the hole, from someone in the barrel. As my cock hardened I became more aware of the large butt plug still up my ass.

"You are a good slave boy. It looks like you are beginning to enjoy yourself. I told you we were not going to hurt you. We only want to make you feel good. Now relax while I make love to your beautiful ass."

Butch moved away from my hungry cock sucking mouth. He positioned himself behind me and removed the butt plug little by little. I thought I would cum it felt so good. Once the butt plug was finally out he again licked my asshole, wet his cock, and placed the head of it to the entry of my ass. My cock was still being sucked and loved, but I did not want to cum just yet.

Somehow over the last hour I had changed my mind, I was no longer afraid of being fucked in the ass. Not only did I now lustfully desire his cock to be thrust into me, I really wanted to be his punk boy. Finally I felt his big cock sliding into me. It didn't hurt like I thought it would. It was awesome!

He was too gentle. I wanted to move my ass back to meet him and have him ram his cock all the way into me. Then filling my yearning desire, he suddenly rammed his cock deep into my ass. It was fantastic. He gripped tightly onto my ass cheeks and pounded away at my now willing ass. The grass that I was smoking enhanced the sexual activity. Whatever we were smoking was tops. I really loved this man's cock up my ass. My body quivered with lustful desire. I wanted him to fuck me, and fuck me hard and rough.

Butch pumped his cock into my ass with perfect precision: like that of a well-oiled piston in the ship's engines. He fucked me long and hard for about 10 minutes. I could feel his body preparing for an incredible orgasm. He became like a wild man, pumping harder and more violently. He slapped my ass several times causing me to tighten my ass muscles. Butch muttered obscene words at me, calling me his whore, and ass slut, pussy boy while pumping load after load of hot manly sperm into me. I was his for the breeding.

My cock was still being sucked by the barrel cocksucker and I was ready to release my load. I couldn't stop now if I wanted to. I gave him my load as he swallowed my cock deep into this throat at the same time as Butch was pleasuring himself in my asshole. I could feel streams of his gushing cum shooting into me. It was awesome.

Butch fell forwards over my body after he shot his load. I felt weak with pleasure and did not want him to pull his impaling cock out of my ass. I wanted his load to stay with me, but as he pulled his cock out of me, some of his overflowing load ran down my balls to the inside of my thigh. My cocksucker friend in the barrel licked up the cum as it oozed down my balls. It was magnificent. I almost fell asleep, but someone started licking my asshole again and sucking the juices out of me. I liked the feeling of being reamed and cleaned out, but also liked the thought of Butch's cum remaining in me. I was so relaxed from my last orgasm that I was about to go to sleep.

My ass-licking friend left me and another body was about to fuck my asshole. I had to admit I was now captivated with the pleasure of something or someone up my ass. I wanted to get fucked again and again. He forcefully entered me and started to fuck me. Butch was standing by my face revealing his beautiful flaccid cock, the cock that had just deposited a fantastic load of sperm up my ass. He knelt down beside me and kissed me on my cheek, then my mouth and warmly kissed my lips as I welcome the stranger's cock into my receptive ass.

"Are you all right?" he asked as he looked at me with concern.

I nodded, then he kissed me again. I had never kissed another man before but I found it was nice. I was now taking a stranger's cock up my ass and I found it was exhilarating to be used like this. I had become a whore slave to receiving cock. My body was their receptacle to receive man sperm.

My cock remained constantly hard. My cocksucker friend had left my cock hanging in the hole and another mouth had replaced him. This cocksucker was using a different method but it was good too. I didn't think I could cum right away but I still enjoyed the feeling of being sucked and fucked at the same time. There was nothing I could do anyway. I was at their mercy. I was being used any way they wanted to use me, and I loved it.

My present ass fucker was about to cum. He breathed heavily a few times, came up my ass, paused briefly, pulled out, then reverently leaned over, kissed my used ass and left me open and ready to have another firm dick fill me again. Once again, I had someone's cum load in my ass. I continued kissing Butch and enjoying this uninterrupted sex. Another ass fucker gripped my buttocks and positioned his cock directly into me with one swift shove. His cock was somewhat bigger than the last one and he vigorously took control.

I shuddered at his sudden move but I had learned how to control my insides and make myself tighter so they could enjoy fucking me. He responded with a hit on my ass and moaned with delight.

Soon, his thick man meat was releasing his juices into my hole. I was getting gang fucked and found it very exciting and a huge turn on. I was now a man whore, and I was ecstatic. I was obsessed with being fucked and used by other men. I loved this man-to-man sex. If my buddies on the ship could be here, they could share my pussy ass and my cock as well. I took another smoke of Butch's joint and continued to kiss him. He stood up beside me and I started sucking on his cock. His semi-hard cock had the taste of his remaining cum on his cock after he fucked my ass. I sucked away and found I was enjoying the cocksucker still sucking on my cock.

I could feel my cock getting harder so my hole tightened up even more causing my present ass fucker to shoot his load into my ass. He pumped such a huge load that it trickled out of my ass. As soon as he pulled out, someone started sucking the juices out of me again. He continued until he sucked most of the cum, then he entered me with his cock. I think he was even larger than the last one, but perhaps my asshole was getting more sensitive. Whatever the size, I still liked it. He would pull it almost all the way out, and then plunge it into me. He lasted for some time before he finally began to cum. He deposited another nice warm load of sperm into my asshole then he slapped me on the butt. After he pulled out, he bent over and kissed my ass. My ass had never been so loved and appreciated before.

My cock was feeling good again and I knew I would soon cum again for the fourth time. No one was fucking me for this moment so I thought it was over, but then I heard the sound of several men gasping as someone walked up behind me again and placed his hand on my hips and his finger to my hole. He slowly moved to me and then I felt a different sensation. His cock must have been very large. He started to place the head of his cock into me. It was big, but I knew I had to take it. I tried to relax. He started in slow and then pulled out. Then he put it back and held his cock to my hole and pushed until the head was in my now-stretched hole. It took some time, and effort, but he got it in me and then plunged all the way to the hilt. I cried out because of the pain but it still felt good in me. I felt crammed with his huge cock. I could not describe the feeling. He let me relax then he started to move.

I continued to suck on Butch's cock. It helped me to forget the pain that I first felt as that big cock entered me. Butch seemed to be in control so I didn't worry.

My cock was being sucked with full stokes while I sucked on Butch's cock as my ass was being fucked by a huge cock. He was big and tall as well as hung like a horse. It had to be at least 12, 13 inches or even bigger. He placed his strong hands on my shoulders and started pumping my ass. He would slap my butt several times while fucking me. He fucked in a very professional way. He sensed that I wanted to satisfy his needs. I loved the feeling of his large hands on me and the sensation of his big balls popping against my balls. He was about to cum. He pumped into me like a stallion horse as Butch was pumping into my mouth and my cocksucker was sucking frantically on me. We were all about to cum.

Butch was starting to cum in my mouth and my cock was starting to cum as my ass fucker pumped his huge load into me. I was drinking down my first load of cum and enjoying every drop. It tasted good and I wanted it all.

Butch place a small vial to my nose and told me to inhale. The smell was awful, like sweaty gym socks but it was such a rush. My cock started cumming as my ass was being filled with gushing loads of manly cum. I felt dizzy but happy. I don't recall what happened but I blacked out.

When I woke up I had been taken from the barrel and placed on a leather-covered mattress on the floor. I was feeling fair enough but tired. I must have fallen asleep but as I looked up into the light above me I saw 6 men standing over me; one at my head, one between my legs, and two on each side of me. The light behind their heads made it difficult to make out their faces. They were dressed in leather and western gear. They all had their cocks out and were starting to jack themselves off. I tried to get off the mattress but Butch was holding my shoulders down. Then he whispered to me:

"They are here to show their appreciation for the night's entertainment so lay back and enjoy a nice cum bath."

I lay back, not only because I was tired, but I knew I had no other choice. I was their body slave, their receptacle for sex and I had to, no, I wanted to do their bidding.

I lay there naked watching these good-looking hunks jacking off their cocks. One of the men placed his boot to my mouth and told me to lick it. I did as he requested. None of the men's cocks were under 7 or 8 inches in length. They looked down at me like I was a god ready to take their offering. I felt my cock twinge as I looked more carefully at each one.

They started jacking off slowly at first then faster and faster as they looked at me and watched each other as they manipulated their cocks. I didn't realize there were so many different shaped and size cocks but I was fascinated and ready for their offering of cum.

I was getting hot as they looked down on me. I started to get hard and found myself jacking off in unison with them. This really turned them on, and as I got harder, they started to cum, one after another. I opened my mouth hoping to catch some of their cum directly into my mouth. I was beginning to love the taste of man cum. I closed my eyes and found myself licking and sucking up their loads of squirting cum as they shot warm manly sperm all over my body and face. I lapped hungrily at the man juices as it shot all over me. I rubbed the fresh cum over my chest and stomach and then I shot another load. One man fell to his knees in the excitement and licked on my balls, while the others finished their loads all over me.

They milked down their last drops of love offering to me. There were a few moments of silence then they began composing themselves during their last moments of pleasure. They placed their cocks back in their pants and left me covered with seven wonderful loads of cum. I continued to lick off the remaining cum from my fingers and fell asleep in the sweet cum bath.

I woke after a short nap as I was being picked up bodily, still naked, and sticky with cum. I was moved to a large area and placed on a small plastic covered mattress. In walked 6 more good-looking men dressed in military uniforms including a policeman and a fireman. I wondered if they were going to shoot more cum on my cum covered body too. Their cocks remained concealed but one by one they took out their cock and aimed them at me. I suddenly realized what this scene was going to be when one man started to piss on me. I didn't know if I was ready for this so I turned my head. They did not aim at my face but seemed to wash off my body with their warm piss.

At one time I think all 6 of them were pissing on me at the same time covering me from neck to toe. I sat quietly and began to enjoy the warmth of the piss. One police uniformed man then aimed his piss stream directly at my face. I closed my eyes as it splashed on my head and ran down my face and into my mouth. I slowly opened my mouth to taste beer-flavored urine. It was surprisingly sweet. I thought he had finished pissing until he grabbed the back of my head and forced his cock into my mouth and let out one more stream. He told me to swallow. I tried to struggle but I was just too worn out to fight back. I swallowed. He had marked his territory and he was happy.

They all finished pissing then shook their cocks as though I was a urinal then left. I sat there in their piss but for some reason it did not bother me. In fact, I noticed I had a semi-hard on. Now I had almost experienced everything.

The lights dimmed in the room and 2 men came over, lifted me up from the bed of piss, and took me into another room. I heard the water of a shower running. I gladly walked into the shower to refresh and clean myself off. It was great and very relaxing. I took a long quiet shower and put on a white bathrobe hanging on a hook and flopped down on the bed nearby and crashed.

When I woke up Butch was sitting by my bed with his hand on my arm.

"Good morning, my young man. How are you feeling today? I have some breakfast and coffee over on the table. We have cleaned and pressed your clothes and they will be here in a few minutes. You slept for almost 10 hours."

I could not believe I had been asleep for 10 hours but I guess I did have a good workout. I was surprised to find that I was not sore anywhere. Even my cock felt like it could go again.

"I have really been asleep for 10 hours?" I asked Butch. "Was that all a dream or did it really happen?"

"It was for real. Would you like to do it again?" Butch asks me. Then he laughed.

"I have something I want to talk to you about. I know we caught you off guard and you probably thought we were going to harm you, but as you can see, you came out of it all right. I hope you are not angry with me. I was thinking we could do some business together if you are interested. What do you say?"

"What? I should be fucking mad at you. You scared the shit out of me several times. However, like you said, you did no real harm to me. What kind of business?" I asked.

"Let me explain last night. I abducted you to put on a sex show. They all paid to watch our show and to watch you being used for pleasure. Now don't get upset but we had an audience of 40 men and they paid for the entertainment. I do this once a month and last night's show was exceptionally good. I try to plan it well so everyone has a good and I might add, safe time." I was stunned. To think I was on display for 40 people and I felt rather humiliated and used. But…what did he have to offer me?

"What did you have in mind?" I ask.

"All right here it is. We had 40 men that paid $100.00 to watch the show. That's $4,000 and you shot a big load for your solo number, that's $100.00 extra. 5 men at $100.00 each fucked you and an extra $50.00 for the big one that made you black out. He measures in at 13 inches, by the way. There were 6 men that paid an extra $10.00 to cum on you; six men paid $15.00 to piss on you, that's another $140.00. My expenses for rental were $250.00. That makes a profit of $4,800. Half of that goes to you, so you made $2,400 for one night's entertainment. How does that sound?"

"I don't know what to say. I am stunned and amazed. Although I could use the money, besides I have to admit, it was fun. My dick isn't even sore and I think my ass might me numb for a few days but…Hummm? Let us get one thing straight. I didn't like the pissing that much, so we have to charge more for that scene, and you must fuck me at least one time and I get to suck you off once during the night."

Butch laughed and laughed and grabbed me and hugged me tightly as I sat next to him at the table.

"About the 'sucking of my cock'. You need a little more practice so we could start on that right away." He laughed again and kissed my forehead.

I stayed with Butch all morning and late into the evening. He was a great guy. He didn't have to share this with me, besides I might have done it for nothing after I got to thinking about it. We drove around the city and we had lunch at a great place near the piers. We made arrangements to meet again next weekend for another night of entertainment. He gave me $2,400 dollars in cash and took me to a bank where I deposited it into my checking account. He said I could stay with him at his place when I came ashore. We became good friends that day. I had to go back to the ship that evening. I know I would look at life quite a bit differently now that I had experienced man love. I would no longer ever call another man a fagot or queer.

As I approached the ship my other 3 buddies were on the dock. They looked like Hell warmed over. They all had hangovers, their clothes were messy and stained, whereas I was all 'spit and polished' and had a big smile on my face, and I might add, money in the bank. They looked at me in wonderment as I walked quickly by them.

"Ahoy mates. Did you get laid?" They gave me a contemptuous look and gave me thumbs down.

Then I laughed and walked up the gangplank looking forward to entertaining again next weekend.

To be continued...

Here is a sample from another story you may enjoy:

"Nothing pleases me more than to satisfy a man that enjoys a good performance..."

DICK CLINTON

Construction Workers

Intense Gay Erotica

I WOULD often visit the Adult bookstores and theaters along Telegraph Avenue in downtown Oakland, California. There was always a variety of gay, bi-sexual, and straight men, searching for quick satisfying sex. Nearly all of the places had an assortment of glory holes, and someone eagerly waiting to service your cock, or wanting to be serviced.

One afternoon, as I was making my customary rounds, I spotted a straight looking hunk going to the back rooms to one of the booths. It was late afternoon when most men had just gotten off work, and were looking for a quick blow job before they went home to their wife and family. I followed him to the back room. After my eyes became adjusted to the semi-dark room, I started looking around for this hot guy. . .

I surmised he must be a construction worker because of the way he was dressed, in his scruffy work boots, faded blue jeans, held up by a large belt, a Dockers work shirt, and a Raiders ball cap on his head. He had a couple days of unshaven beard and had a thick soiled blond mustache on his upper lip. He looked to be about six foot four inches tall, and weighed a solid two hundred ten pounds of hard solid man.

I quickly acquired a roll of tokens for the movie booths and went to the back room. He was standing by the movie selection area looking for a good movie to view. Immediately, four other men were in pursuit of him. He was a man's man. I discovered during my cruising years, it was not wise to be too forward to most straight men. It could be a turn off, so I waited and played it coy. He studied the movie selection on the wall then headed towards one of the booths for viewing. He turned and glanced back at me and then went inside one of the movie booths, shut and locked his door.

Before he could even sit down, two hungry fags rushed to the adjoining booths on each side of him. "Damn." I said to myself. "I lost that one quickly." but thought I would wait around, hoping he wouldn't like the movie and move to another booth. The movie soon stopped. He came out of the booth, and back to the movies selections where I was still standing. Then he spoke to me in his deep masculine voice.

"Fuck. These movies are lousy. I have better ones at my pad. My name's Terry. Here's my address. Bring over a couple 6 packs of Bud and be there in about 20 minutes. It'll be worth your time." He said. Then he turned and left me standing there with my mouth ajar.

I was stunned but quickly came back to my senses, and left the bookstore. I went to the liquor store nearby to pick up a six pack of beer, hopped in my car and headed to the address he gave me. I was familiar with the area and soon found the address. It was in a low-income housing development, clean but small apartments. I quickly found his place and apprehensively knocked on his door. I heard a voice say, "Yeah, Yeah, Yeah! Hold on to your jockey shorts. I'll be right there!"

The door opened and there stood my construction hunk, almost nude except for a jockstrap. He motioned for me to come in. I followed him in thru the small hallway to his living area. I was admiring the view of his firm buttocks framed in the straps of the jock. He quickly stripped out of his jockstrap, flopped down on the couch, adjusted his balls and said to me, "Well? Where the hell is my beer? I could use a cold beer right now. I worked hard today. Pop one open for me buddy, then get yourself over here and kneel between your man's legs. Enjoy sucking my big cock while I relish your warm mouth on my meat," he shook his large flexible cock at me.

The TV was on, and he was watching his 'fuck films' on the VCR. He was a hot looking masculine and demanding stud. I had experienced this type of treatment before by the two city motorcycle cops that lived in my apartment. I realized it 'turned me on'. I was to do his bidding and satisfy him without question. It could be dangerous going to a stranger's apartment, but I had good judgment about my partners. This guy was big and strong and could probably snap my neck with one twist, but underneath this hunk, I sensed a gentle man. He needed to be in control, and pursue sexual pleasure whenever he needed it.

As I looked around the room, I observed a framed picture of a woman on one table. Perhaps his ex-wife. His furniture was anything but feminine. An overstuffed leather couch and unmatched lounge chair filled the small room along with a twenty one inch TV, an end table with a lamp, and a floor lamp in one corner. It was obvious he had lived in a larger place before moving here.

Obviously when he came home from work he stripped, and dropped his clothes on the floor and on the end of the couch. He had tossed his sweat stained jockey shorts on the floor next to his feet, and his dirty socks lying across his work boots by the other chair. His faded work jeans were over the arm of the chair and his belt was touching the floor. A couple empty beer cans set on the floor next to an ashtray with a half smoked cigar...

He had medium length sun streaked blond hair. His large muscular shoulders and upper forearms had some sort of military symbol and on the back of one hand was a small blue star. I'd noticed earlier he had a pair of bright red lip prints tattooed on one of his buttocks. I wasn't much for tattoos but whoever did the artwork on him did a good job. Some guys look hot with tattoos and Terry was one of those guys.

The scent of manly body sweat is often like an aphrodisiac during sex to many people including me. His scent was more like the combination of a vanilla-almond aroma. Perhaps it was his chemical balance. I positioned myself on the floor between his legs…

If you enjoyed this sample then look for <u>Construction Workers</u>.

Also by this Author

Hard Pounders in Tight Quarters

Safekeeping

Butch Trade

Pleasant Encounters and Adventures of Corey

Cop Sucker

The Beach House

Boarding House for Men

Adventures at the Lake

Community Service

Main Attraction

Farm Boy Mischief

About the Author

I was born in our family home in 1935, after the depression and before WWII, in a small township called Shawnee, Kansas.

After College I joined the US Navy for four years. Soon after I was honorably discharged from the navy, I met my first gay male companion and lived with him for four more years in Kansas. During that time, I worked as an Accountant and part-time Professional Male Model for a commercial photo studio for Sears, JC Penny, Goodyear Tire and Tasty Milk Company.

I was offered a job at Denver Business College and worked as an assistant for two more years. During my spare time I attended Barber and Cosmetology Academy and received my state license. I achieved first place as top Stylist of my class, and received a two weeks paid scholarship to Hollywood Beauty College in CA.

After my Hollywood experience I went to Scottsdale, AZ and worked as a style director at Sacs Fifth Ave Salon, until I became allergic to the chemicals I was using and had to resign.

I became active politically in San Francisco and in Metropolitan Community Church of SF and was ordained as Head Deacon for life by Elder Rev. Troy Perry of Los Angeles, CA and can legally marry, perform Baptism and give Holy Communion in the state of California.

I lived, worked, and played in the SF Bay Area until I retired in January 2000 and moved to Surprise, Arizona. I began writing erotic stories after I moved to Arizona. My stories have been published in Handjobs Magazine and by other Blogs on the Internet.

I now live in a home on a Senior area of Arizona where I write and enjoy the warm weather of the Arizona sun.

Check my page on Amazon for Updates and interesting info.

Author Central Page - http://amzn.to/1aGgEt5

If you enjoyed any of my books then please share the love and click like on my books in Amazon.

If you write me a review and send me an email I will send you a free book, or many.
(Just know that these emails are filtered by my publisher.)

Good news is always welcome.

One Last Thing, For Kindle Readers...

When you turn the page, Kindle will give you the opportunity to rate this book and share your thoughts on Facebook and Twitter. If you enjoyed my writings, would you please take a few seconds to let your friends know about it? Because... when they enjoy they will be grateful to you and so will I.

Thank You!

Dick Clinton
dick_clinton@awesomeauthors.org